The Path to
Snowbird Mountain

THE PATH TO SNOWBIRD MOUNTAIN

Cherokee Legends by TRAVELLER BIRD (Tsisghwanai)

FARRAR, STRAUS AND GIROUX
NEW YORK

Copyright © 1972 by Traveller Bird
All rights reserved
Library of Congress catalog card number: 70-183741
ISBN 0-374-35757-9
First printing, 1972
Published simultaneously in Canada
by Doubleday Canada Ltd., Toronto
Printed in the United States of America
Designed by Cynthia Basil

CONTENTS

Introduction   3

 1 The Place of the Beginning   11

 2 How the Animals Obtained Fire   17

 3 Thunder Appoints
    the Eagle Ruler of Earth   21

 4 The Origin of Corn and Beans   27

 5 The Legend of
    the Cherokee Sweet Shrub   33

 6 The Squirrel and the Crawfish Race   39

 7 Why the Possum's Tail Is Bare   43

 8 The Dog and the Hunter   47

 9 How the Raccoon
    Got Rings on His Tail   51

10 The Rabbit and the Honey-Gum Slide   55

11 The Terrapin and
    the Possum Outwit the Fox   63

12 How the Rabbit Lost His Eye   67

13 The Man Who Became a Lizard   71

14 The Hunter, the Ukten, and Thunder   75

15 The Panther and the Crow   79

16 The Seven-Clan Scribe Society   83

The Path to
Snowbird Mountain

Introduction

A series of mountains rise out of the great Appalachian Range in Graham County, North Carolina, southwest of the Great Smoky Mountains. For my people, the Eastern Band of Cherokees, it is an old, old landmark, and they gave it the name Snowbird Mountains because it is said that long ago there once lived on the highest peak a giant white Snowbird who was the grandfather of all the little snowbirds we see today.

To me, this region is the top of the whole world—the land of the Sky People, it was said. The skyline is in all directions and close at hand. It is a land of cold, rushing rivers, small creeks, deep gorges, dark timber, and waterfalls. Great billowing clouds sail upon the mountains and in early morning a blue-gray mist hangs just above the treetops. Winter brings ice and snow. Spring and summer, a profusion of colors. The white Cherokee rose tipped with pink is the first flower to bloom. Then from the Earth Mother come the purple violets and brown, sweet-smelling sweet shrub. Still later, the mountains flame in orange and yellow honeysuckle and red and white rhododendron.

My grandfather lived near the headwaters of Snowbird Creek and he lived to be very old. His name was Sigigi. He was my mother's father. When he was born, in 1866, the majority of the Cherokee tribe had been forced by the United States government, more than a quarter of a century before, to remove from their ancestral homelands to the West. But small groups of little more than 1,300 Cherokees defied the United States government and its army and refused to leave their lands.

In the fall of 1838, when government troops began driving the Cherokees from their homes to the white man's stockades in North Carolina and Tennessee, Sigigi's grandfather Ogan and three others escaped from Fort Cass and fled to a cave in the Snowbird Mountains. Hundreds of other panic-stricken Cherokees also managed to elude the soldiers, seeking refuge in other caves in the Smoky Mountains.

For weeks, these Cherokees were hunted like animals by men who used dogs to track them and fire to destroy the mountains and their food supply.

After a compromise was reached with the United States government, the Cherokees remaining in North Carolina were permitted to live in their mountains on lands Will Thomas, a white man, purchased for them with their money. He held the deeds for the Cherokees. But for thirty-eight years the Eastern Cherokees lived in constant fear of eviction.

From birth, my grandfather knew the pain of defeat of his divided people and the deep yearning of the old warriors. As he grew up and endured, he refused to yield his own secret soul and birthright to his enemies. And in this, there was a quiet courage and pride, knowing in the whole who he was.

Although my grandfather lived out his long life in the shadows of the Snowbird Mountains, his memory was like the continuous flow of a stream that reached out over the immense landscape of our people. He could tell of the Western tribes whom he had never seen, and the great plains and deserts where he had never been. He never learned to read and write the English language.

Grandfather Sigigi's house was two rooms made of notched logs. Spaces between the logs were chinked with red mud. At the east end of the largest room, there was an outside chimney made of small poles and red mud baked like red pipestone. Inside, the fireplace was built of large, flat stones. The house was built high enough up the slope of Little Snowbird Ridge so that its residents could overlook the narrow valley and winding path leading to the highest peak. Grandfather had chosen this site for his home because he liked being able to look far away and because the narrow valley and high mountains gave a feeling of security.

There were a lot of sounds in my grandfather's house, a lot of coming and going, feasting and talk. The summers were full of excitement. Reunions with kinsmen from nearby Indian communities and from far-off Oklahoma and Mexico brought on a time of festivity. The aged kinsmen who came to my grandfather's house when I was a child were made of sinew and leather. They wore black hats and bright-colored, hand-made shirts. The women wore long, flowing cotton dresses, bead-work, and scarves tied around their heads. The women exchanged gossip in soft tones, while the men made jokes, gestured with their hands, and laughed a lot.

When I was a child, I played with my cousins outside where the light from the great cooking fires fell upon the ground, and the talking of the old people echoed away in the valley. There were a lot of good things to eat—a lot of special little treats, for my grandmother and her women helpers were excellent cooks.

When the weariness of play overcame us children, I lay down on a quilt pallet with my cousins and listened to the katydids and the croaking frogs away by the creek, and felt the cool wind blowing against my cheeks.

The stories and legends in this book are the path to Little Snowbird Ridge, where as a child I listened to tribal stories told by my aged grandfather.

"They say this was the way it was . . .
a long time ago . . ."

1
The Place of
the Beginning

The mystic seven-pointed star represents the sky origin of the Cherokees and indicates their separation into the Seven Clans.

The early Council House had seven sides. There were seven major festivals in the year, the seventh being celebrated only every seventh year. The Foundation of Life, which is the Cherokee National Ritual and the most sacred, must be repeated seven times in succession by seven priest-physicians who represent their respective clans. And there are seven colors, whose magical symbolism is associated both with compass points and human qualities.

The Eternal Fire was fed by seven different varieties of wood, which represented the contribution of the Seven Clans.

From my grandfather, I was told the Beginning:

"Now, you know this was the way it was a long time ago. The Old Ones say that the Tsalagi [Cherokee] came down from the sky. It is said the People descended from Eagles. This is what the Old Ones tell of the beginning."

A long time ago all was water. The animals lived in Galulati (above). This is the Highest Place, because it is measured to be seven hand-breadths above the Earth, or the Seventh Height—far out past the Sky Vault.

But the animals were crowded and wished more

space to walk around in. It appeared something must be done or in a very few harvests there would be standing room only. The animals wondered what was below the water. So the Eagle called a council of all the animals—all that flew, all that walked on four legs, and all that crawled. It was decided that they would let the Turtle go and see what was below because he was such a good swimmer and carried his house about with him.

The Turtle jumped down into the water and swam in all directions, but could not find a solid place to sit down. He decided to dive down to the bottom and see what was down there. So the Turtle dived down, and he went so fast that he hit his head on a rock, flipping over on his back. When he turned himself over on his four legs, he found that his back was covered with soft mud, which began to grow and grow as he swam up from the bottom, until it was an island by the time the Turtle reached the surface of the water. This island is what we now call Earth.

The animals looked down from Galulati and saw what happened to the Turtle. The Turtle called out to them and said, "I'll make my home in the waters. Now, tie up the four corners!"

Gananesgi (Spider) spun four strong cables from Galulati to the four corners of the Earth, so that it would not become lost. Today, because of the Turtle and Spider's good work, we have the Earth. The Turtle lives in the water. Spider continues spinning her cables here on Earth.

In the beginning, the Earth was wet mud and flat country. The animals in Galulati were anxious to get there, so they sent different birds down to see if the Earth was drying. But the birds found that they all mired up in the soft mud. So the only thing to do was to wait.

After a long, long while, the Eagle said he thought the time was just right and he would go and get the Earth ready for them. This was the Great Eagle, the father of all eagles we see today. He flew all over the Earth. He was very fast. He pivoted and rolled, and swung downward, his great wings and tail fanning the Earth. Then he glided upward, riding on the cold columns of air. The Earth was still soft mud. Now the Eagle was particularly curious about one area. He flew down lower to examine it more closely. Wherever his wings fanned and struck the mud, there was a deep depression, a valley. And when he soared skyward, there were mountains.

The animals watched the Eagle prepare the Earth for them. When they saw so many mountains on the Earth, they became afraid the whole Earth would be mountains, so they called to the Eagle and said, "We cannot all live in mountains. Fly lower! Fly lower!"

14

Now to this day the old Eastern Cherokee country is full of beautiful mountains, called the Great Smokies.

2
How the Animals
Obtained Fire

The Cherokee's was a water culture. While Sun and her alter ego, Fire, played a vital role in our culture, it was Water, the life-giver, who had first place in Cherokee ritualistic structure. No medicine was more powerful; no ceremonial rite more sacred.

The River, the line of life, whose head is at the highest mountaintop and whose foot stretches away to the lowest valley, is called Yunwi Ganohidv (Long Man, or Long Human Being). He moves along eternally, the rippling of the stream and the roaring of the falls speak in unknown tongues to the Old Ones only.

When the animals came down to Earth, there was no Fire and all was cold. Thunder, who lived in Galulati toward the west, heard the animals talking about how cold it was. So he struck a high peak on the island, causing a large hole, where he put Fire.

The animals saw smoke coming from the hole and wished they could get the Fire. So they held a council.

First the Eagle said he would go and get Fire from the hole, for he was so swift that he thought he could bring it back in a gourd, which he tied to his neck with a vine. But when he got to the Fire hole and attempted, with his beak, to dip the gourd down into the Fire for coals, his feathers and beak were scorched black, and the gourd burned up. So he returned without the Fire.

Next the Crow said he would go and try to get the Fire. The Crow took a long stick in his beak and flew over to the Fire hole. He stood on the brink of the hole and put the dry stick down into the Fire so that it would burn in the flames. When the stick caught afire, he pulled it out with his feet, but the flames from the stick burned his feet and the smoke from the hole scorched his feathers. He failed and flew back without the Fire.

The next two birds which volunteered to get the Fire from the hole were the Buzzard and the Turkey. But the same thing happened to them that happened to the Eagle and the Crow. They were burned black.

Then the Rat said, "I will go. I can dig underneath the ground and bring Fire back on my tail." But when he dug his path under the Fire hole and tried to put hot coals on his tail, the hot ashes smoked him gray, and the hair on his tail was burned off. That's why the Rat has a slick tail today.

All the animals so far had failed to get the fire.

Then Thunder spoke to the animals. He said, "I will send my son, Tagv (Firefly), to get Fire."

The little brown and yellow striped fly sped over to the Fire hole. When he got there, he burst the hole open and scattered the Fire. Then he disjointed his body and put a coal of Fire inside, jointed himself together again, and flew back with the coal of Fire inside him. He then unjointed himself and placed his coal of Fire inside a dusdia (small clay bowl). While he was unjointing himself, a tiny piece of the coal broke off, but Tagv didn't know it when he joined himself together again. That's why the Cherokees call the Tagv (or Firefly) the Lightning Bug, for he is the son of Thunder and it was he who went and got Fire for the animals.

3
Thunder Appoints the Eagle Ruler of Earth

I have known of eagles, our sacred keeper of the land.

One May morning when I was eight, I went with my father and grandfather to Snowbird Peak. The clouds hung low on the mountaintop. They were white and billowy and it seemed that you could reach right up and touch them.

While we stood there looking out over a timeless landscape of iron mountains and budding timber that stretched away into the four cardinal directions, we saw two eagles flying over the canyons in the distance. They would soar in wild and silent flight, and then swing across the blue skyline, spinning and spiraling. They were Bald Eagles, a male and a female. My grandfather said they were in their mating flight. They were exciting to watch; free and just beautiful.

L ong ago when the Earth was new and all things could talk, Thunder went searching for his friend, the Eagle. Thunder was the Ruler of all the Universe, and the Eagle was his best friend. Thunder found the Eagle sitting on Looking-Glass Peak. They had a conference.

Thunder said to the Eagle, "I appoint you Ruler of all the animals. You are to rule over all creatures that fly, all creatures that walk on four legs, and all creatures that crawl on Earth. You must have a council with all the wild animals. You must ask them what they want to be able to do, and you must grant them their request if you think it right they should be that way. You are to be my helper on Earth."

So the Eagle called a council of all the animals. They met in the animal council house on Little Snowbird Mountain. All kinds of birds came, and all the four-legged animals, and the animals that crawl.

When they arrived, they took seats on logs in the council house. Each tribe was assigned certain seats. The Eagle stood near a small fire in the center of the council house. He asked each one of them what he wanted to be able to do.

The Yellow Mockingbird (huhu) stood up and said, "I want to be a learner. Can you give me the power to sing all the songs of the other birds, so that when a person hears me sing he will think there are many birds around?"

The Eagle said, "Well, if you wish to be that way, I guess so."

That is how the Mockingbird got his power to imitate all the songs of the other birds.

The little Chickadee (tsidilili) got up and said, "I would like to be a fortuneteller. When people are to have visitors, I want to go and give them a message ahead of time. This I can do by flying to a tree near their house and singing a beautiful song.

23

Would you give me that power?" the Chickadee asked.

"Yes," the Eagle said.

That is why the Cherokees say when they see a chickadee fly into a tree near the house, that someone is coming.

Then the Frog (walasi) got up and went and stood by the Eagle. "See these bumps on my body? People are always stepping on me and causing me to have sores. Could you give me the power to blow myself up so that when a person sees me, he will instantly die of fright?"

"No," the Eagle said. "You are too small. I could not give you that power. But I will do this—I will let you jump a long distance, and when a person sees your blown-up body jump, he will become frightened."

The Beaver (doi) got up and said, "I want to make a poison that will kill people because they take my coat. Can you give me that power?"

"No," said the Eagle. "But I will give you sharp teeth like a knife to bite them with."

"All right," the Beaver said.

Next the Cat (sahoni) stood up and said, "I want to be a great magician, a nightwalker, but I cannot see when the Sun goes to sleep. Will you give me the power to see in the Nightland?"

The Eagle said, "I guess so."

24

That's why the Cherokees say when they see a cat walking in the darkness, that he is a night-walker.

Then came the Redbird (totsuhwa), the beautiful singing bird. He got up and said to the Eagle, "I want to be a truthteller. Let the people trust me. I want to sing joyful songs when it's going to rain."

"All right, you can have that power," the Eagle said.

That is why the Cherokees believe that when they see the beautiful redbird sitting in the top of a tree it will rain.

The Grasshopper (sigigi) said, "I want to be an expert singer and dancer. When people hear me sing and see me dance, they will laugh and become happy."

So the Eagle gave that power to the Grasshopper.

This is what my grandfather Sigigi said the Old Ones told long ago of how the Eagle became the Ruler of the Earth and gave power to the other animals.

4
The Origin of Corn and Beans

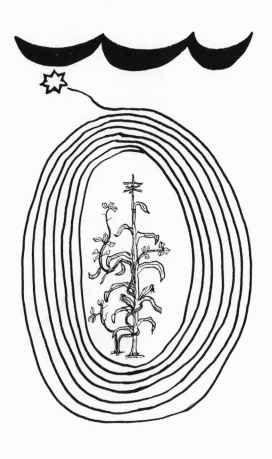

Corn and beans are the Indian's staff of life. American Indian researchers have found that two-thirds of the world's foods came from the native peoples of North and South America. Medicinal herbs which the Indians have used since ancient times are still used today both by Indian physician-priests and by non-Indian chemists and doctors.

Often, my grandmother made corn meal and grits by pounding the corn in a kanon (wood mortar) with a heavy long wooden pestle.

The Old Ones say that a long time ago, when the Earth was new, there was a woman called Selu Tvya who lived alone in the shadow of Looking-Glass Mountain.

One day at sunrise, while on her way to the spring, she saw a clot of blood beside the path. She carefully covered it with a cucumber leaf. On the seventh sunrise, she removed the leaf and found a boy baby. She took him home and raised him as her own, and he called her Grandmother.

When the boy was seven years old, Selu Tvya made a bow and arrow for him and sent him out to hunt game. The boy learned all about the animals and birds that were good to eat. But his grandmother told him nothing about plants, and as time went by, he became more and more curious about the corn and beans that she prepared for their dinner.

28

So one day the boy followed Selu Tvya when she took her basket and went to the unwatali (storage house). Peeking through a crack between the logs, he saw her leaning over her basket. She rubbed the right side of her body and corn spilled over into the basket. Then she rubbed the left side and beans poured out. The boy was frightened and horrified. He was convinced that his grandmother was a witch and that he should kill her.

When Selu Tvya returned to their cabin, she noticed the strange look on the boy's face, and she guessed he had found out her secret. She knew what he was thinking. At that moment, her nose began to bleed and she knew that she was going to die. She said to the boy, "When I'm dead, clear a lot of ground on the south side of the cabin. Cut off my head and put it on a pole. I'll help you watch. Drag my body over the ground seven times. You must stay awake all night and keep watch; in the morning you will have a great supply of ripened corn and beans. Do not close your eyes for even a moment, for if you fall asleep, the corn and beans won't grow."

After she died, the boy cut off her head and placed it on a pole overlooking the fields to help him keep watch. Then he began to clear the ground, but it was hard to do because there were so many trees and brush and tangled vines to be removed. Finally he cleared seven small patches. If the boy had cleared a lot of ground as he was instructed, corn and beans would grow throughout the world. But they grow in only a few places, because that was how the land was cleared.

The boy dragged Selu Tvya's body around the small patches of ground twice only, instead of seven times as he was told to do. And this was the beginning of the Cherokee custom of working the corn and beans only twice during the growing season.

Wherever a drop of blood fell on the right side of the boy, a stalk of corn sprouted. And when a drop of blood fell on the left side, a bean plant sprang up. That was the beginning of the custom of the Cherokees of planting the corn with the beans.

The boy stayed up all night watching the corn and beans grow, and at sunrise they were fully ripened. To the boy, it seemed that each cornstalk was wearing a skirt of Earth; and to this day, one must prepare the Earth-skirt before planting the seed, which is believed to be the old grandmother, Selu Tvya.

When the nearest villagers heard about the new grains that could be made into bread, grits, hominy, soup, and other wonderful foods, they came and asked the boy for some seed. The boy gave them seven grains of red corn and seven brown bean seeds, and showed them how to plant them. He explained that the villagers must stay awake all night to grow seven ears of corn and seven bean vines by morning. But the journey back to their village was a long one. The sun was hot and the path dusty. The people planted the seven corn and seven bean seeds, but one by one the tired villagers fell asleep. By morning the seeds had not even sprouted. The magic spell was broken; no longer would corn and beans mature overnight.

The Cherokees have called these gifts of Selu Tvya (Corn Bean) by her name ever since that time long, long ago.

5
The Legend of the Cherokee Sweet Shrub

Like most Indian tribes, the Cherokees were a divided people after the European invasion. There were five distinct groups of the People. Each group had its own chosen leaders.

My grandmother's name was Wadulisi (Honey). She was a member of the Mexican Cherokee group. In 1895, when she was nineteen, her parents returned to the old Cherokee country to recover buried tribal records and to visit clansmen. While there, Wadulisi married Sigigi. Since she was their only daughter, her parents decided to settle in the Snowbird Community on lands of kinsmen.

Long ago, the Old Ones say that in the year of the Great Harvest, the land of the Cherokees was becoming too thickly populated. The people realized that they needed more lands in order to grow and prosper. So the Peace Chief sent out a delegation of the leading men of the nation to talk with the neighboring Anitsigsu (Chickasaws), who claimed large areas of suitable lands toward the southwest.

Now the Chickasaws were not as strong as the Cherokees, for they had been at war for a long time with their enemies.

The Cherokees sat in council with the Chickasaws to arrange the terms of the exchange of territory. This council lasted for many days. There were many courtesies to be observed before business could be started. At the beginning, it was polite to sit in complete silence. Then the didahnvwisgi (physician-priest, commonly referred to as "medicine man") enacted the lengthy invocation. After the invocation, the ancient and sacred Tsola (tobacco) Pipe Ceremony must be performed.

The Pipe was passed leisurely around to each council member, who took his turn on the sacred medicine. Some elaborate speeches of greeting and the presentation of gifts expressed the good will of the visitors. These were answered by the hosts. These amenities must not be hurried, lest it appear that the Cherokees were eager to have their business done with and go on home.

At the end of each day, the Chickasaws prepared an elaborate feast, which was served by the young maidens. The most beautiful maiden of them all was the daughter of the Chickasaw War Chief.

Among the Cherokee group was Sanuwa (the Hawk), nephew and heir of one of the powerful Cherokee War Chiefs. The first night he sat for a long time around the campfire composing a love song. The next afternoon he did not appear at the council meeting. He was playing the new song on his flute near the cabin of the Chickasaw Chief.

The Chickasaw maiden heard Sanuwa's love song and she secretly went to meet him by the bend in the river. They enjoyed the thrill of a forbidden adventure. They gathered wild flowers and waded barefoot across the stream, following after the shrill cry of the blue dove. Sanuwa told her of the land of his people, where the mountains touch the sky and the sun always stands still. He knew that he was expected to choose a wife from the proper clan of an important Cherokee village in order to increase the power and solidarity of the nation. And she, too, knew that a brave warrior had spoken to her parents for her. But the Redbird Spirit of love pays no heed to the notions of nations, and fluttered at the breast of the young lovers.

So the young lovers agreed that when the council was ended and his people went on their way homeward, Sanuwa would come for her. They planned that if he should be detained she would hide in a thicket at the bend of the river and he would come for her there.

Finally the council ended between the Chickasaws and the Cherokees. The Chickasaws agreed to move back a day's walk to allow for the expansion of the Cherokee Nation, and to share their hunting lands with the Cherokees.

Many of the Chickasaw warriors objected to the trading away of their lands and wanted to fight for them, but the Civil Chief could see that there was no chance of keeping the land for themselves. He argued that it was better to trade it away than to lose it, along with the lives of many warriors.

But when the Cherokees left, the daughter of the Chickasaw War Chief could not be found. The Chickasaw warriors began a search for her. They were the first to find her, hiding in the thicket at the bend of the river.

When Sanuwa arrived, he found her dead. He buried her there at the bend of the river. Then he rejoined his own group and began the long journey homeward.

The next spring, Sanuwa returned and found among the deep green leaves growing over the mound the soft brown petals of a sweet-smelling bush. He knelt beside it and called it his Sweet One, for he had claimed the Chickasaw maiden for his own. He carried the bush back to his homeland and planted it. But, long before the long winter was over, he grew eager to see and to be with his Sweet One. So he went back to her grave and waited until his own death came.

But the bush with the deep brown flowers spread throughout the lands of the Cherokees. And to this day, the Cherokee Sweet Shrub opens her eager face and sweet smell in early spring to welcome the return of her loved one.

6
The Squirrel and the Crawfish Race

I went swimming in Snowbird Creek on summer afternoons. It was a secret place, enclosed by a thicket of white rhododendron and spruce growth.

The pool of white water was cool and clear. Once, from the edge of the sandy bank, a huge old crawfish watched me as I swam. His eyes popped out from his head and his long canoe-shaped body was a dull brown. His pincers were the largest I had ever seen.

There is something awesome about crawfish. They stop and stare, and then go on, dragging their canoes upon their backs.

O ne day the Crawfish was out of the river and playing around in the wet sand near the riverbank. A Squirrel was sitting near him. They began to talk and walk very fast upon the ground.

The Crawfish said, "I can run very fast. If I had to run a race, I could do it right now."

The Squirrel said, "What can you do to run a race? You're so slow—you just crawl upon the ground and drag your canoe upon your back."

"Well, if you don't believe me, I'll run a race with you," said the Crawfish.

"All right. Let's run a race," said the Squirrel.

So they got up and went to the top of Snowbird Mountain, from where they would have to go down and up, down and up, seven times.

To start the race, they stood even with each other on a broken limb of a tree. Both whooped as they started, and the Squirrel's tail flipped right by the Crawfish, who grasped the end and got upon it.

The Squirrel was racing as hard as he could, but he was really the only one in the race because the Crawfish was riding on his tail. When they got to the seventh ridge, the Squirrel whooped, and right beside him whooped the Crawfish.

The Squirrel said to the Crawfish, "You sure are fast!"

"I said I was. I'm very fast. I race lots of times with many animals bigger than me," said the Crawfish.

The Squirrel said, "We'll race seven more times."

So they turned around and ran again. The Crawfish got upon the Squirrel's tail as the Squirrel whooped and flipped his tail to start the race. When they arrived at the seventh ridge, the Squirrel whooped, and right beside him whooped the Crawfish.

On their seventh round, about halfway, the Crawfish nearly fell off the Squirrel's tail, and he decided to seat himself more firmly. While he was trying to seat himself better, he accidentally grasped the bony part of the Squirrel's tail with his pincers.

When they arrived at the seventh and last ridge, the Squirrel whooped, then turned around to the Crawfish and said, "You're cheating me!"

"No, I'm not," said the Crawfish. "That's how fast I am."

The Squirrel said, "I felt it when you pinched my tail. I knew you were back there riding."

So they went around and around and around, the Squirrel chasing the Crawfish. But the Crawfish couldn't get away. At last the Squirrel plunked his tail down upon the Crawfish and flipped him up in the air just as a Duck came flying over. The Duck caught the Crawfish in his beak and ate him.

7
Why the Possum's
Tail Is Bare

The stories my grandfather told were old and sacred, and they meant a great deal to him. He saw our culture almost destroyed and he wanted to preserve it.

At a very early age he taught me how to listen. He led me into the presence of his mind and spirit and I shared in the wonder and beauty of his thoughts that were eternal to him. Nothing of his great age or of my childhood came between us.

A long time ago, the Possum used to have a long, fluffy tail. He was always singing and dancing about his beautiful shiny tail, and bragging to the other animals about his good looks. This made all the other animals jealous and they hated the Possum.

Now the Rabbit, who was very clever, decided to play a trick on the bragging Possum.

There was to be a council the next day and all the animals had to be present. The Rabbit was the message runner. It was his business to inform all the animals of the meeting.

So the Rabbit went to the Possum's place in a persimmon tree, and told him of the meeting. The Possum said he would come if he could sit with the Chief so that all the other animals could see his handsome tail.

The Rabbit said that it would be all right. The

Possum could sit with the Chief. But the Rabbit thought that he ought to send a hairdresser to dress the Possum's tail for the council meeting.

The Possum said, "All right."

The Rabbit went to the Katydid and said, "The Possum wants you to come and dress his tail for the council. Pretend you are combing his tail, but you must really cut all the hair off. You take this skin that the Snake shed, and wrap the Possum's tail so that it will stay smooth and fluffy until the council meeting."

Now the Katydid's tail is like a knife, and this is what he would use to dress the Possum's tail with.

So that night the Katydid went to the Possum's place and said to the Possum, "Rabbit said you wanted me to come and get your tail ready for the council."

"Yes, that's right," the Possum said.

"All right, then, you can just lie over there in the grass and close your eyes; stretch your tail out so that I can comb it. I'll sing you a song while I work," said the Katydid.

The Possum lay down and stretched himself out on the grass. He closed his eyes while the Katydid began to comb out his tail and sing. But all the time the Katydid was combing the Possum's tail, he was really cutting off all the hair near the roots with his tail, and the Possum never knew it. As the Katydid combed the Possum's tail, he wrapped the Snake skin around it to keep it smooth and shiny until the council the next day.

The next day the Possum went to the council house and sat on the log next to the Chief, the Bear, just as the Rabbit promised him he could do. When it came the Possum's turn to make a talk, he loosened the Snake skin on his tail and walked to the middle of the floor. The Possum began to talk to the animals and gesture with his hands while walking back and forth before everyone, swinging his tail low to the floor. As he swung his tail, the loosened Snake skin came off, and as it did, all the hair fell off the Possum's tail.

Everybody began to laugh and clap his hands.

This pleased the Possum, so he talked and walked and swung his tail faster and faster. But the animals laughed so hard and long that the Possum wondered why they were laughing at him. Then he looked down at his tail and saw that it had no hair on it. It was as slick as a lizard's tail. He was so ashamed and disturbed that he could not say another word. He grinned and said, "He!" and fell over on the ground as the Possum does today when he is taken by surprise.

8
The Dog and the Hunter

My grandfather always had dogs around his place. They were free and trusted friends. Some were huge, and all had black spots above each sleepy black eye. A dull black line ran the length of each of their backs. This is a story Grandfather told once when I was about nine.

Once there was a Hunter who lived alone in the mountains. His wife and children had been killed by enemies while he was away hunting. Game became very scarce, and this forced the Hunter to travel far, looking for food. Now, it was dangerous to be alone, for there were many enemies around.

So the Hunter took his bow and pack of arrows and walked far into the wilderness looking for game. He shot a buffalo with his last arrow, but the buffalo was only wounded and ran off. The Hunter wondered what to do, for he heard the enemy all around him. He could think of no way to escape from them.

Then the Sun spoke to the man, saying, "Your brother is just up ahead, near the mountaintop. Go there and he will help you."

The Hunter started walking up the mountain path, and met a Dog trotting toward him. The Dog stopped and said, "Friend, you have enemies close by and around you. I have some puppies. They are motherless and weak. I have no milk for them. If you will take care of my puppies, I will be your brother and helper. I will lead you away to safety."

The Hunter said, "I will take your puppies and care for them."

"Lend me your clothes," said the Dog. "You can go stay with my puppies in my cave until I return."

So the Hunter took off his clothes and the Dog put them on and became just like a man.

The Dog went to where the Hunter's enemies were, and they began shooting and chasing him. The Dog, looking like the Hunter, dodged and outran the enemies' bullets and led the Hunter's enemies to a swamp where there was quicksand. The Hunter's enemies began to cross the swamp and they all became mired in the quicksand and died.

Then the Dog went back to his cave, where his puppies and the Hunter were waiting. He took off the Hunter's clothes and gave them back to the Hunter, who put them on again.

The Dog said, "We can go now. Your enemies will not bother you again."

The Hunter took the four weak puppies and wrapped them in his hunting shirt to keep them warm. Then the Dog led the Hunter around and around toward the Hunter's home.

While they were walking along the path by a river, the Hunter saw the buffalo which he had wounded with his last arrow. The Dog pulled out one of his whiskers, which instantly became an arrow, and gave it to the Hunter. Then the Hunter took careful aim and shot the buffalo. He cut off the hide and much meat. Building a fire, the Hunter, the Dog, and the puppies feasted on buffalo meat.

Afterwards, wrapping much of the meat in the hide, the Hunter carried it on his back and the puppies in his arms, and the Dog led the way to the Hunter's home.

9
How the Raccoon Got Rings on His Tail

One summer morning when I was seven, I went to a higher peak above Grandfather's house to dream up a new song. As I was lying on a boulder, humming to myself, a raccoon came out of her den in a red-oak tree above me and watched and listened. In a while, she came down the tree and walked out a little way in front of me and began singing also:

> *U na ko la ti   e la wo ge quu*
> *I go gwo du u hi   do ti gwa la sgu*
> *Gu wa du hnu u hi   i gu gwo du u hi*

A translation goes like this:

> *I am beautiful!*
> *Like the yellow Rainbow,*
> *From my feet up,*
> *I am beautiful.*

One day the Raccoon met the Terrapin, who was wearing some pretty yellow rings around his neck, and the Raccoon wanted them. But he didn't know how he was going to get them away from the Terrapin. Then the Raccoon began thinking—he thought of a plan. The Raccoon said, "Those rings sure look funny on your short neck. Let me show you how to wear them."

"You might run off with them," the Terrapin said.

"No, I won't. You can stay here and watch me," said the Raccoon.

"Well, I guess it'll be all right," the Terrapin said.

So the Terrapin took off the seven small yellow rings on his neck and gave them to the Raccoon, who put them on his tail.

"Now I'm going to walk over there so you can see how these rings look on my tail," the Raccoon said.

The Raccoon walked a small distance from the Terrapin, and turned around, swinging his tail back and forth and up and down. Then he asked, "How do they look on me?"

"Just fine. They look good on your tail," the Terrapin said.

Then the Raccoon began to dance and swing his tail. He danced faster and faster and farther and farther away from the Terrapin.

The Terrapin hurried to catch up with the Raccoon and called out, "You thief! Bring my rings back to me!"

But the Raccoon broke into a run and ran up a tall oak tree that had a hollow, leaving the Terrapin on the ground.

That is how the Raccoon got yellow rings on his tail and why he lives in a hollow of a tree to this day.

10
The Rabbit and
the Honey-Gum Slide

The People (American Indians) have always helped each other. This is our tribal way of doing things.

Often on the reservation my people had a gadugi. A gadugi is a group of unpaid workers called together to donate their services for the common interest of the community.

A long time ago there was a drought. All the rivers, creeks, and springs dried up and the animals had no water to drink. This was when all the animals could talk.

So the Eagle and his Assistant Chief, the Wolf, called a meeting of all the animals—all that flew and all that walked on four legs. Then the chiefs talked to them.

"We don't have any water to drink. Now we are going to hunt for water. We are going to have a gadugi. We will dig a spring when we find damp ground," said the Wolf. All the animals thought this was good and were glad to help—all except the Rabbit.

Now, the Rabbit is tricky and is very proud of his clean coat. Every day he takes a dust bath in powder dirt. He wears a white tie and white gloves on his hands, and he doesn't like to get his feet dirty.

The Rabbit was thinking of a way to keep from working and dirtying his coat. He told the other animals, "I don't need to dig a spring. I get all the water I need by putting my gourds out at night under the trees. The dew from the leaves fills them up by morning. Goodbye! I'm going to hunt strawberries."

Then all the animals said, "If you won't help us dig, you shall have none of our water. Don't you come stealing our water!"

"Well, I don't need your water," the Rabbit said.

So all the animal workers began to hunt for damp ground. The Honeybee was the first to find a damp spot, by a huge beech tree. She began to dig for a spring, and the other animals came and helped her. They dug down deep into the ground before they found water seeping up through the dirt. While the water was seeping through, the animals lined their spring with stones, and made stone steps down to the water so that they would have a way to get down and up.

After the spring was finished, the Rabbit saw all the animals going to get water there, and he began to think of ways to steal their water.

One morning before dawn, he took his small gourds with handles and went to the spring while all the other animals were still sleeping, and got some water. Each day for three days, the Rabbit stole water from the animal spring.

On the fourth day, the Bear was passing by the

Rabbit's house and stopped to see how he was getting along. The Bear saw the Rabbit's gourds of water sitting on shelves and asked, "Where did you get so much water?"

"I told you! I put my gourds out at night; in the morning they are full of dew. Then I take them home to use."

Now the Bear didn't think much of the Rabbit's water story—he just didn't believe the Rabbit. So he returned home, and along the way he told all the other animals that he met about the Rabbit and the many gourds of water sitting on shelves in his house.

The animals all said, "I bet he's stealing our water. Let's go see about our spring."

Each of the animals went to the spring and walked down the stone steps to the water. There they found the Rabbit's tracks.

"That Rabbit's been stealing our water! Let's punish him! We'll trap him when he comes again!"

"How?" asked the Wolf. "He's very clever."

The animals thought and thought of a way to trap the Rabbit. Then the Honeybee said, "Why not pour some of my honey on the stone steps, and when Rabbit comes for water, his feet will stick to it, and we can catch him."

"Yes, that's good. We'll put some pine gum with the honey so that Rabbit will remain stuck," said the Bear.

"All right," they agreed.

The Honeybee and her helpers flew off to her bee-hive in the sycamore tree, and the Bear took cucumber leaves and filled them full of pine gum. The Honeybee poured her honey on the stone steps and the Bear came and poured his pine gum over it, making the steps very sticky and slick.

Just before dawn, the Rabbit went to the spring to get some water. He went down the stone steps and felt the sticky gum and honey on his feet. "What is this?" he said to himself. About that time, his feet slipped out from under him and he slid into the water. The Rabbit swam around and around and around in the water, trying to jump out on the sticky stone steps. Every time he would jump out, his feet would slip and he would fall back into the water.

Finally he began to whoop for help. "Help me, I'm drowning! Come get me out of here, I'm freezing!"

The Owl was listening and watching for the Rabbit. She heard him yelling and flew off to inform the other animals that the Rabbit had been caught in the spring.

All the animals came and looked down into the spring, where they saw the Rabbit swimming around and shivering in the water.

So the Wolf got a long grapevine and dropped it down into the spring and told the Rabbit to hold on to it while he pulled him out of the water. When the Wolf pulled the Rabbit to the top of the spring, the other animals grabbed him and tied his legs with the vine. Then they carried him to the council house.

At the council house, the animals discussed what to do with the Rabbit. "Let's cut his head and legs off," they said.

The Rabbit thought this was funny. He laughed and said, "I take my head and legs off every night before I go to bed."

"Let's build a fire and burn him," the animals said.

"I can kick the fire to pieces and put it out," the Rabbit said.

"Well, what can we do with him?" the animals asked.

"I know! Let's throw him in the briar patch where the wasps have their nest of young. The wasps will sting him and that will take care of Brother Rabbit," said the Fox.

"That's it! That's what we will do," they all agreed.

Then the Rabbit began to cry. He bawled louder and louder. "No! Don't do that to me! Please don't do that. I hate briar patches; briars tear my beautiful coat," the Rabbit cried.

But the Rabbit was thinking to trick all the other

animals, for he really liked briar patches. He knew that he could run away as soon as they threw him in.

The Wolf took the Rabbit's front legs and the Bear took his hind legs and they swung him up high into a big thick briar patch.

When the Rabbit landed in the briar patch, the wasp nest was shaken and they flew around and around over the head of the Rabbit, who was lying on the ground, kicking off the vine that bound his legs. When the Rabbit kicked himself free from the grapevine, he whooped and whooped, then ran zigzagging away.

11
The Terrapin and the Possum Outwit the Fox

On early mornings in late summer, I went with my grandmother to gather papaws. I climbed the papaw trees and shook the smaller limbs so that the yellow, fragrant fruit would tumble down to the ground. Then my grandmother and I gathered it in her hand-made, river-cane basket. My grandmother made delicious pies, jelly, and candy with this tasty fruit.

The Terrapin and the Possum like to eat the same kinds of foods, so they decided to be good friends and help each other out if one of them was caught by enemies.

Now the Possum was a great magician. In the pocket in her breast where she carries her young, she also carried a bone whistle so that when her children were outside sunning and playing she could blow the whistle and call them back to her.

The Fox likes to eat terrapins and is always trying to catch them. Now, the Possum hated the Fox because he was always bragging about his beautiful coat and long, bushy tail.

One day the Possum invited the Terrapin to go papaw-hunting with her. They went down to a creek where there were many papaw trees. The Possum climbed up the papaw tree while the Terrapin waited in the grass on the ground. As the Terrapin was waiting for the Possum to throw some papaws down to her, the Fox slipped up behind the Terrapin and caught her.

He was about to kill her, when the Terrapin asked, "Are you hungry?"

"Yes," the Fox said.

"Well, before you eat me—my friend Possum climbed this papaw tree and has some papaws for me to eat. If you like, you can have some to eat too."

"Well, all right! I'll see how I like papaws," the Fox said.

When the Possum was ready to throw down the papaws, the Terrapin said, "Let's play a game. The one who is quicker will get the fruit."

"All right," said the Fox.

Six times the Possum threw papaws down and the Fox rushed to get them.

The Fox said, "I sure didn't know papaws tasted so good!"

The seventh time the Possum threw down a papaw, she stuck her bone whistle inside the soft fruit. The Fox quickly ran to catch the papaw in his mouth. As he ate it, he swallowed the bone whistle, which stuck in his throat, and he couldn't breathe.

That is how the Possum tricked the Fox and helped her friend, the Terrapin, avoid being killed and eaten.

12
How the Rabbit
Lost His Eye

The Rabbit was always playing tricks on his wife. This sometimes made the Rabbit's wife angry and she pouted.

One day the Rabbit wanted his wife to cook some peas, but she was pouting and refused to let him have any. So he said, "Well, if you won't let me have any peas, I'm going to the ball game. But, before I go, I want you to know that our old Chief One-Eye will come by today and you must cook dinner for him. You might cook him some peas. When he finishes eating, tell him to come over to the ball game."

The Rabbit left, and when he had walked a little way from his house, he sat down on a log and took out one of his eyes and put it in a hole in the log. He sat humming to himself a little while, then he went back to his house.

When he came to the door of his home, he knocked and his wife came to the door. Thinking her husband was Chief One-Eye, she bowed and said, "Chief One-Eye, come in. My husband told me you were coming by. He has gone to the ball game. You must eat dinner. I have it ready on the table. I've cooked your favorite food—peas."

So the Chief, who was really her husband, seated himself on a reed mat and Mrs. Rabbit set down a bowl of peas for him to eat.

"These peas sure are delicious. Peas are my favorite food," Chief One-Eye said.

This compliment pleased Mrs. Rabbit, so when the supposed Chief One-Eye finished eating the first bowlful of peas, she gave him another and another to eat. He was truly fed all the peas he wanted.

After the Chief had eaten all the peas that he wanted, he washed his hands and face, spitting on his pads and wiping his face and ears.

"Well, I guess I'd better go on over and see the ball game," said the Chief.

He left and ran back to the log where he had left his eye. When he got there, he couldn't find his eye. The Crow had stolen it and taken it far away and dropped it in a creek.

The Crow sat in a tree nearby, laughing. He said, "Ghoga! Ghoga! Now you are a One-Eyed Rabbit. Ghoga!"

The Rabbit cried and cried. But his tears could not bring back his eye that the Crow stole and lost.

So the Rabbit went back home and his wife said, "Where's your eye?"

"I was playing stickball at the ball game; they hit me in the eye and knocked my eye out forever."

The Rabbit wanted everybody to believe that he lost his eye in the ball game. But he really lost his eye by taking it out himself and pretending that he was Chief One-Eye.

13
The Man Who Became a Lizard

In his middle years, my grandfather was a didahnv-wisgi, which is both physician and priest. He spoke a language all his own and carried a sacred buckskin medicine bundle no one was allowed to open. He knew and saw things that other men did not know and see. His magic incantations had great power and he knew the names of all the wild plants and the curing properties that they possessed.

Once, when he was a boy, my grandfather went with his grandfather Ogan to a deep pool on the Nantahala River to fish. As they were sitting on a large rock near the riverbank, the water suddenly rose. Then there began an awful thrashing below the surface. They looked down into the deep clear pool and saw a huge lizard-like animal that had a head like a man. They became afraid and ran away.

A long time ago there were two brothers who lived with their grandmother. It was winter and game became scarce. There was no food. So the brothers went out into the woods to hunt.

All day they walked and walked, but could find no game to kill for food. Late in the evening they came to a river and decided to rest and camp for the night. They built up a fire and lay down to sleep.

During the night, one of the brothers was awakened by a crawling noise. He got up and found fresh meat there on the ground by the fire. He was very happy and excited. He awoke his brother and said, "Come look at all the fresh meat someone has left for us. Now we have plenty of food."

But his brother was afraid and replied, "It is a strange thing. I believe we should not eat that meat."

His brother laughed at him and told him he was foolish to believe that way. He went ahead and cooked some of the meat and ate all he wanted by himself. Then he lay down beside the fire and went to sleep.

Later in the night, the brother who had not eaten the meat heard thrashing about, and looking over to where his brother was, he saw that his body was beginning to change to that of a large lizard. The changed brother spoke. "Your thinking was right. You must not eat that meat. Now I'll have to go and live in the water, but we are brothers and I want you to come and see me now and then."

After that, he crawled away from the fire and went down the bank into the river. Oftentimes, the brother went down to the water's edge and called his lizard-brother out and told him how things were with the Cherokees.

14
The Hunter, the Ukten, and Thunder

The Cherokee language is hard to understand, but we know Thunder understands it. Thunder is the Ruler of all fierce things in the Universe, and Lightning and the Rainbow are his beautiful robes. He provides the rains and he overcomes the strong winds.

Long ago a Hunter went out to hunt for game with his bow and arrows. This Hunter always brought home something good to eat.

One day he was going home with some rabbits and squirrels that he had shot, and he saw a pretty Ukten (snake) lying on a rock by the trail. The Ukten had bright colors and seven spots on its head. It looked lean and hungry.

The Ukten called out to the Hunter, "Would you find me something to eat? I'm very hungry. I eat birds and rabbits."

The Hunter felt sorry for the Ukten and threw it some rabbits and went on home.

A few days later the Hunter came by with some quail and a deer, and he saw the Ukten again. The Ukten seemed friendly and had grown quite a bit. "You and I are friends," the Ukten said.

So the Hunter gave the Ukten several quail to eat.

Sometime later the Hunter came by again and brought some turkeys and squirrels for the Ukten. This time the Ukten had grown very large.

The Hunter said to him, "You sure are getting big and fat."

"Yes," said the Ukten. "That's because you bring me good things to eat. You and I are friends—we'll be friends always."

So the Hunter went on home. That night the people of the village were having a Woman's Dance, and all the people from the neighboring villages came. They were going around the fire, dancing and singing the old songs, when the Hunter looked up and saw the Ukten coming down the mountainside.

The Ukten was now so big and long that he stretched out a far distance. He was covered all over with pretty colors and he had seven horns on his head. From his mouth, he was sputtering smoke and fire and building fires as he came on toward the people's village.

Now the people saw the Ukten and the fires that he was building, and they were very frightened. They wondered what to do.

Then a very strange thing happened. As the Ukten came off the mountainside, closer and closer to the people, the people heard a low thundering. As the Ukten crossed the valley toward the village, it began to coil itself around something. The people saw that it was Thunder.

Thunder called out to the men of the village, "My nephews, this Ukten that is coiled around me kills

77

people. Shoot him on his seventh horn. It is there that you must aim your bow and arrows."

But the Ukten said, "Don't do it! Kill Thunder, he is fooling you. His blast will kill you."

Then Thunder said, "This large Ukten is tricking you. He wants to kill you. I am your friend and helper. Help me, my nephews!"

So the men believed Thunder. They told some of the boys to get their bows and arrows and to shoot the Ukten on the seventh horn.

The boys got their bows and shot together and hit the Ukten on the seventh horn. It fell over dead and Thunder was freed from its coils.

When Thunder was free, he began thundering and making rain to put out the fires that the Ukten had built. Since that time long ago, Thunder and the people have always been friends and have helped each other.

15
The Panther
and the Crow

Some of my earliest memories are of the summers on Little Snowbird Ridge, where we lived in a log house a few yards above my grandfather's place. From there you could look down the narrow valley to Grandfather's apple and plum orchard. When the fruit became ripe, it looked like round coals of red fire. Beyond, there was Snowbird Creek and the long sweep of the larger Snowbird Mountains as they stretched away in the four cardinal directions.

The Panther and the Crow are enemies.

One day the Panther saw the Crow washing himself in a creek. Quietly the Panther swam out under water and caught the Crow by the legs. "Now I'm going to have a crow dinner," the Panther said.

"Before you eat me, let me dance for you," said the Crow.

"No," the Panther said. "You might fly off."

"Well, if you won't let me dance for you, let's have a contest. Let's have an Eating Contest," the Crow suggested. "I always carry a bag of food with me."

"All right. Just you don't fool me," said the Panther.

Now, the Crow is a great magician. He picked up two leaves with his beak and they instantly became wooden bowls. Then he put some food, from the pouch under his throat, in the dishes, and sat down with the Panther to eat.

While eating, the Crow put his food back into his pouch, but the Panther didn't know this. He just kept on eating.

When the food was all eaten up, the Crow put more in the dishes, and they continued eating. The Panther began growing bigger and bigger. He said, "I think I'll get a drink of water. Don't you fly off!" He got up and wobbled to the creek bank and began drinking water.

The Crow was thinking. He said, "Look, yonder come some hunters!"

This frightened the Panther. He forgot all about the Crow and dived into the creek. And being so full of food and water, he was unable to swim. He drowned.

The Crow flew away. He won the contest.

16
The Seven-Clan
Scribe Society

The legend of the Seven-Clan Scribe Society was my grandmother's story. It is a true legend and a beginning of Cherokee history. This legend has appeared in print only once before, in my biography of my blood ancestor, Sogwili, known in history by the names Sequoyah and George Guess.* But it is well known among our fullblood, traditional people from North Carolina to Mexico. And the Cherokee Scribe Society was no secret to the European invaders, or to the colonial government.

Most Indian tribes had pictographs and hieroglyphs—symbol writings of their tribe in their own particular style and language. Indians, of course, had an oral history, but we also had a written one, which the conquerors carefully concealed in order to exploit Indians and their country.

Long before the fifteenth century, the Cherokees were just one of the Indian tribes who used a codex with hieroglyphics. Nine years before Columbus landed on San Salvador Island, chosen Cherokee scribes were writing and reading in their native ninety-two-symbol syllabary.†

Because of their knowledge of the Cherokee tribe's literacy, the United States government forced

---

* Bird, Traveller, *Tell Them They Lie: The Sequoyah Myth.* Los Angeles: Westernlore Publishers, 1971.
† A system in which written characters represent syllables, not letters as in an alphabet.

upon the Cherokees its "great experiment"—that is, assimilating or "civilizing" the Indians into the white man's culture and life style. But many of the Cherokees resisted and refused to yield their own culture for that of the foreigners.

You might have heard or read the story of how George Guess, known as Sequoyah, invented the Sequoyah syllabary so that his people could become civilized. This is a fallacy that conceals a conspiracy and true Indian history. My blood ancestor was a revolutionary. He used the syllabary to block the progressive movement carried out by the missionaries and leaders of the Cherokee Nation to change Indian culture and language.

Sequoyah's real name was Sogwili, meaning "Horse" in Cherokee. He was a fullblood Cherokee-Taliwa-Tasgigi Indian. His formal or English name was George Guess. He was a warrior and scribe of the Seven-Clan Scribe Society. Beginning in October 1795, he taught the traditional ones the syllabary so that they could outwit the United States government's civilization program and retain their native culture and life ways. He was my grandmother Wadulisi's great-grandfather.

The Seven-Clan Scribe Society was an important organization of the Cherokee tribe. Its members were direct descendants of those old men and women of the Taliwa who had made the journey along the edge of oblivion. It was a society that stood apart from the others in certain ways. This difference, this superiority, had come about a long time ago. Long before the white man came, there was received into the population of Sogwiligigagei-hiyi (Redhorse Place, a Cherokee village in the mountains known today as the Great Smokies) a small group of immigrant Indians from the southwest.

The immigrants were a wretched people, for they had experienced great suffering. Their lands were the plateau country of the Great Plains, and for many years thieves and hunters had taken a toll of the people. At last they gave themselves up in despair. Their spirit broke. But it was not a human enemy that overpowered them—it was famine. No rain fell. Springs and creeks dried up in their canyons. Crops failed and game left their lands. Thousands of the people died, and the tribe teetered on the edge of oblivion. Fewer than twenty-five survivors remained in the end—fourteen women and ten men.

One day the priest-physician went out alone to pray and to look for food. He walked seven days. On the seventh day he came to a canyon that had high red walls. Thunder cracked and Lightning flashed in the sky, but there was no cloud. A voice spoke to him: "What is it you hunt?"

86

The priest-physician said, "My people are hungry. Most have died."

The voice said, "Go to your relatives in the Great Mountains to the east. Follow me!"

There was a sudden sunburst across the blue sky —a red beam lay from west to east. It withdrew slowly like stars receding in the dawn.

The Taliwa walked. It took more than a year to reach the mountain valley of Sogwiligigageihiyi. It is said that the great-great-great-great-grandfather of Sequoyah's mother went out with a delegation to welcome and escort the Anitaliwa into their village.

The ragged group brought with them little more than the clothes on their backs, but even in this moment of deep hurt and humiliation they brought, of themselves as a people, one great gift—the thin gold plates bearing their written language. Now, after the intervening years and generations, the ancient blood of this Indian tribe still runs in the veins of men of the Seven-Clan Scribe Society.

This is how the Cherokee tribe obtained its written syllabary with six different dialects of the language, and ninety-two symbols representing the syllables.